Daniel San Souci
Country Road

A Doubleday Book for Young Readers

A Doubleday Book for Young Readers
Published by
Delacorte Press
Bantam Doubleday Dell Publishing Group, Inc.
1540 Broadway
New York, New York 10036

Library of Congress Cataloging in Publication Data
San Souci, Daniel.
Country road / Daniel San Souci.
p.   cm.
Summary: A walk with Dad along the old country road one day in spring brings
sightings of a hawk, fox tracks, a school of trout, and other signs of nature.
ISBN 0-385-30867-1
[1. Nature—Fiction.   2. Animals—Fiction.]   I. Title.
PZ7.S1946Co   1993   [E]—dc20   92-8379   CIP   AC

The paintings for this book were done in Winsor & Newton watercolors
on 140 lb. hot press watercolor paper.
The typeface is 16 point ITC Berkeley Old Style Medium.
Typography by Lynn Braswell
Manufactured in the United States of America
October 1993
10   9   8   7   6   5   4   3   2   1

For Brian and Angela Bischoff

$\mathcal{E}$arly one Sunday morning in spring my dad and I went for a walk. Behind us, smoke from the last of Grandpa's winter firewood drifted from the farmhouse chimney into the wind. Above us flew a flock of crows, cawing loudly. I didn't feel much like going on a hike when the house was so warm and cozy.

"It seems like only yesterday I was your age, walking on this road through puddles," Dad said, "and making the biggest splashes I could." Today the ground was hard and dry. The morning air had a wintry chill, but Dad didn't seem to notice.

"This old road is full of life," he said. "Look at these wildflowers. It's going to be a colorful spring."

Suddenly I saw Grandpa's German shepherd, Bluebell.
Long legs pounding, tongue flapping, she came bounding
toward us at full speed. I hoped she'd keep us company, but
after a bit she got bored and tore back toward the meadow.
Dad smiled and said, "We're just way too slow for that dog."

"Not me," I yelled, and ran partway up the road. Suddenly I stopped and stood still. A red-tailed hawk was perched in the big oak tree. It shifted from one talon to the other, watching me. You never see anything like that in the city.

I heard Dad's footsteps behind me. "Shhhhh," he whispered. "Don't make any fast moves." We stared at the hawk for a long time, until it lazily lifted its wings and rose into the sky.

We came to a trail branching off from the road and followed it to a clearing where mounds of dirt were stacked in lines.

"The moles are digging for worms," Dad said, "just like I used to do when I went fishing as a kid." Then he laughed. "I'm glad they're out here. They'd make your grandpa mad if they went worm hunting in the farmhouse lawn!"

We walked back down the trail to the main road. A woodpecker flew across our path. It swooped onto a dead fir tree and began poking holes in the bark.

Dad lifted his binoculars out of his pack and handed them to me. When I looked in them, the woodpecker seemed so close I could have counted every feather on its body. This old road was sure full of surprises.

Farther along, a squirrel in a sugar pine tree started chattering at us. Dad pointed to some faint scratches on a thick tree trunk. "Those were made by a bear, a long time ago," he said.

I asked if there were still bears around here. "Not for years," he said. "Too much building and too many people. They've gone away, and I can't say I blame them."

Around a bend a flock of homing pigeons was using a barn roof for a landing strip. They seemed restless and watched the sky. "That hawk is still around," my father said.

Where a little spring kept the ground damp, we found fox tracks. "There's a chicken coop alongside that barn," said Dad. "I'll bet you that fox has his sights on a chicken dinner."

We reached an apple orchard where the trees were getting ready to bloom.

A family of quail scooted around in the thick underbrush, looking for wild food. I'd blink my eyes and they'd disappear; then suddenly there they'd be again. "Now you see 'em, now you don't," Dad said, laughing.

Beyond the orchard we came to a pasture. Three horses were running and playing, enjoying their freedom after spending the winter in their stable.

I imagined myself riding bareback across the meadow all the way to the far hills. Dad said gently, "Daydreams are as common as weeds along this old road."

We stopped to eat our lunch at a tangle of fallen pine trees. A lizard that was sunning itself raced out of sight. "These trees were washed down years ago in a flood,"

Dad said. "Now they're home to lots of animals." As if to
prove him right, a deer mouse scurried out from between
some branches.

Finally we came to an old stone bridge. Underneath, the water flowed over smooth gray rocks, and a school of trout swam in the deepest pool.

Nearby, a tree frog croaked, answering another frog farther up the river. Dad said, "We're almost at the end of the old road. The new road is just beyond that rise up ahead."

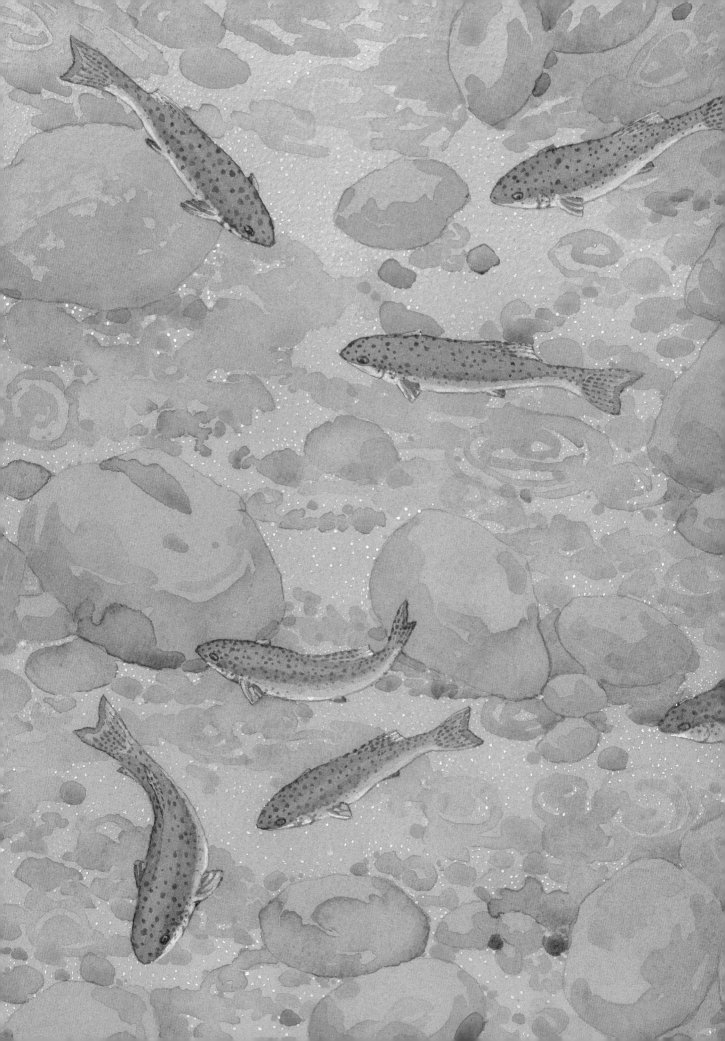

Together we started up the gentle slope. From the top of the rise the winding old road behind us looked as friendly and contented as a cat curled in the sun.

Ahead of us the new road paved with blacktop looked hard and cold. Tract houses crowded against the hills. We stood side by side in silence.

I looked around at mounds of freshly dug earth, and piles of lumber. "What are they going to build?" I asked.

"More houses, more stores," my father answered, frowning slightly.

Then he smiled and said, "Don't worry about our old road. It's weathered an awful lot, and I'll bet it will survive these changes too." I gave him a smile back.

"Well," my father said at last, "it's time to head for home. If you're tired, we can walk along the new road. That will take us back to Grandpa's quicker."

"No, thanks," I told him, "I like this road just fine."

"Maybe we'll get lucky and see that hawk again," Dad said. But I already felt lucky enough just to be on that road, the two of us together.